JACK LONDON ON ADVENTURE

JACK LONDON ON ADVENTURE

Words of Wisdom from an Expert Adventurer

JACK LONDON

Skyhorse Publishing

Skyhorse Publishing books may be purchased in bulk at special discounts for sales promotion, corporate gifts, fund-raising, or educational purposes. Special editions can also be created to specifications. For details, contact the Special Sales Department, Skyhorse Publishing, 307 West 36th Street, 11th Floor, New York, NY 10018 or info@skyhorsepublishing.com.

Visit our website at www.skyhorsepublishing.com.

10 9 8 7 6 5 4 3 2 1

Library of Congress Cataloging-in-Publication Data is available on file.

Cover design by Jane Sheppard

Print ISBN: 978-1-63220-667-1
Ebook ISBN: 978-1-63220-891-0

Printed in China

CONTENTS

THE ARTIST AS ADVENTURER

There is an ecstasy that marks the summit of life, and beyond which life cannot rise. And such is the paradox of living, this ecstasy comes when one is most alive, and it comes as a complete forgetfulness that one is alive. This ecstasy, this forgetfulness of living, comes to the artist, caught up and out of himself in a sheet of flame; it comes to the soldier, war-mad on a stricken field and refusing quarter; and it came to Buck, leading the pack, sounding the old wolf-cry, straining after the food that was alive and that fled swiftly before him through the moonlight. He was sounding the deeps of his nature, and of the parts of his nature that were deeper than he, going back into the womb of Time. He was mastered by the sheer surging of life, the tidal wave of being, the perfect joy of each separate muscle, joint, and sinew in that it was everything that was not death, that it was aglow and rampant, expressing itself in movement, flying exultantly under the stars and over the face of dead matter that did not move.

—from *The Call of the Wild*

You can't wait for inspiration. You have to go after it with a club.

He was justifying his existence, than which life can do no greater; for life achieves its summit when it does to the uttermost that which it was equipped to do.

In a letter to Cloudesley Johns:
A man without courage is to me the most despicable thing under the sun, a travesty on the whole scheme of creation.

And yet he wanted to live. It was unreasonable that he should die after all he had undergone. Fate asked too much of him. And, dying, he declined to die. It was stark madness, perhaps, but in the very grip of Death he defied Death and refused to die.

—from *Love of Life*

Don't quit your job in order to write unless there is none dependent upon you.
Don't dash off a six-thousand word story before breakfast.
Don't write too much. Concentrate your sweat on one story rather than dissipate it over a dozen.

Don't loaf and invite inspiration: light out after it with a club, and if you don't get it you will nonetheless get something that looks remarkably like it.

Set yourself a "stint," and see that you do that "stint" every day.

Study the tricks of the writers who have arrived. They have mastered the tools with which you are cutting your fingers.

Keep a notebook. Travel with it, eat with it, sleep with it. Slap into it every stray thought that flutters up into your brain. Cheap paper is less perishable than gray matter, and lead pencil markings endure longer than memory.

And work. Find out about this earth, this universe . . .

—from *Getting into Print*

I write for no other purpose than to add to the beauty that now belongs to me. I write a book for no other reason than to add three or four hundred acres to my magnificent estate.

Life is so short. I would rather sing one song than interpret the thousand.

In a letter to Ethel Jennings:
You wrote your story at white heat. Hell is kept warm by unpublished manuscripts written at white heat. Develop your locality. Get in your local color. Develop your characters. Make your characters real to your readers. Get out of yourself and into your readers' minds and know what impression your readers are getting from your written words. Always remember that you are not writing for yourself but that you are writing for your readers.

All my life I have had an awareness of other times and places. I have been aware of other persons in me.—Oh, and trust me, so have you, my reader that is to be. Read back into your childhood, and this sense of awareness I speak of will be remembered as an experience of your childhood. You were then not fixed, not crystallized. You were plastic, a soul in flux, a consciousness and an identity in the process of forming—ay, of forming and forgetting.

You have forgotten much, my reader, and yet, as you read these lines, you remember dimly the hazy vistas of other times and places into which your child eyes peered. They seem dreams to you to-day. Yet, if they were dreams, dreamed then, whence the substance of them? Our dreams are grotesquely compounded of the things we know. The stuff of our sheerest dreams is the stuff of our experience. As a child, a wee child, you dreamed you fell great heights; you dreamed you flew through the air as things of the air fly; you were vexed by crawling spiders and many-legged creatures of the slime; you heard other voices, saw other faces nightmarishly familiar, and gazed upon sunrises and sunsets other than you know now, looking back, you ever looked upon.

Very well. These child glimpses are of other-worldness, of other-lifeness, of things that you had never seen in this particular world of your particular life. Then whence? Other lives? Other worlds? Perhaps, when you have read all that I shall write, you will have received answers to the perplexities I have propounded to you, and that you yourself, ere you came to read me, propounded to yourself.

—from *The Jacket (The Star-Rover)*

In a letter to Charles Warren Stoddard, 21 August 1903:
I do not live for what the world thinks of me, but for what I think of myself.

Naturally, my reading early bred in me a desire to write, but my manner of life prevented me attempting it. I have had no literary help or advice of any kind—just been sort of hammering around in the dark till I knocked holes through here and there and caught glimpses of daylight.

—from autobiographic material submitted to Houghton Mifflin and Co.

The thought of work was repulsive. I didn't care if I never settled down. Learning a trade could go hang. It was a whole lot better to royster and frolic over the world in the way I had previously done. So I headed out on the adventure path again.

—from *John Barleycorn*

And while he appeared very sick and looked about him with dull eyes, he noted the fighting strength of Ivan's men, and noted with satisfaction that Ivan did not recognize him as the man he had beaten before the gates of the fort. It was a strange following his dull eyes saw. There were Slavonian hunters, fair-skinned and mighty-muscled; short, squat Finns, with flat noses and round faces; Siberian half-breeds, whose noses were more like eagle-beaks; and lean, slant-eyed men, who bore in their veins the Mongol and Tartar blood as well as the blood of the Slav. Wild adventurers they were, forayers and destroyers from the far lands beyond the Sea of Bering, who blasted the new and unknown world with fire and sword and clutched greedily for its wealth of fur and hide. Negore looked upon them with satisfaction, and in his mind's eye he saw them crushed and lifeless at the passage up the rocks. And ever he saw, waiting for him at the passage up the rocks, the face and the form of Oona, and ever he heard her voice in his ears and felt the soft, warm glow of her eyes. But never did he forget to shiver, nor to stumble where the footing was rough, nor to cry aloud at the bite of the lash. Also, he was afraid of Karduk, for he knew him for no true man. His was a false eye, and an easy tongue—a tongue too easy, he judged, for the awkwardness of honest speech.

But at front and rear, unawed and indomitable, toiled the two men who were not yet dead. Their bodies were covered with fur and soft-tanned leather. Eyelashes and cheeks and lips were so coated with the crystals from their frozen breath that their faces were not discernible. This gave them the seeming of ghostly masques, undertakers in a spectral world at the funeral of some ghost. But under it all they were men, penetrating the land of desolation and mockery and silence, puny adventurers bent on colossal adventure, pitting themselves against the might of a world as remote and alien and pulseless as the abysses of space.

Father must have had strong in him the blood of adventure. He looked upon our catastrophe in the light of an adventure. No anger nor bitterness possessed him. He was too philosophic and simple to be vindictive, and he lived too much in the world of mind to miss the creature comforts we were giving up. So it was, when we moved to San Francisco into four wretched rooms in the slum south of Market Street, that he embarked upon the adventure with the joy and enthusiasm of a child—combined with the clear sight and mental grasp of an extraordinary intellect. He really never crystallized mentally. He had no false sense of values. Conventional or habitual values meant nothing to him. The only values he recognized were mathematical and scientific facts. My father was a great man. He had the mind and the soul that only great men have. In ways he was even greater than Ernest, than whom I have known none greater.

THE INDIVIDUAL PURSUIT OF LIFE

I would rather be ashes than dust! I would rather that my spark should burn out in a brilliant blaze than it should be stifled by dry-rot. I would rather be a superb meteor, every atom of me in magnificent glow, than a sleepy and permanent planet. The proper function of man is to live, not to exist. I shall not waste my days in trying to prolong them. I shall use my time.

—London speaking on living and dying to friends two months before his death, quoted in the *San Francisco Bulletin*

Life is not a matter of holding good cards, but sometimes, playing a poor hand well.

"You can write 'Honorable' before your name," she flashed up proudly. "But my father has been a king. He has lived. Have you lived? What have you got to show for it? Stocks and bonds, and houses and servants—pouf! Heart and arteries and a steady hand—is that all? Have you lived merely to live? Were you afraid to die? I'd rather sing one wild song and burst my heart with it, than live a thousand years watching my digestion and being afraid of the wet. When you are dust, my father will be ashes. That is the difference."

—from *The Turtles of Tasman*

Do you know the only value life has is what life puts on itself?

Query: If a man, with the whole historical process behind him, can create an entity, a real thing, then is not the hypothesis of a Creator made substantial? If the stuff of life can create, then it is fair to assume that there can be a He who created the stuff of life. It is merely a difference of degree. I have not yet made a mountain nor a solar system, but I have made a something that sits in my chair. This being so, may I not some day be able to make a mountain or a solar system?

—from "The Eternity of Forms"

He was mastered by the sheer surging of life, the tidal wave of being, thc perfect joy of each separate muscle, joint, and sinew in that it was everything that was not death, that it was aglow and rampant, expressing itself in movement, flying exultantly under the stars.

In letter to Anna Strunsky:
And how have I lived? Frankly and openly, though crudely. I have not been afraid of life. I have not shrunk from it. I have taken it for what it was at its own valuation. And I have not been ashamed of it. Just as it was, it was mine.

But—and there it is—we want to live and move, though we have no reason to, because it happens that it is the nature of life to live and move, to want to live and move. If it were not for this, life would be dead. It is because of this life that is in you that you dream of your immortality. The life that is in you is alive and wants to go on being alive for ever.

—from The Sea-Wolf

"I have worked hard," Frederick explained to Polly that evening on the veranda, unaware that when a man explains it is a sign his situation is growing parlous. "I have done what came to my hand—how creditably it is for others to say. And I have been paid for it. I have taken care of others and taken care of myself. The doctors say they have never seen such a constitution in a man of my years. Why, almost half my life is yet before me, and we Travers are a long-lived stock. I took care of myself, you see, and I have myself to show for it. I was not a waster. I conserved my heart and my arteries, and yet there are few men who can boast having done as much work as I have done. Look at that hand. Steady, eh? It will be as steady twenty years from now. There is nothing in playing fast and loose with oneself."

And all the while Polly had been following the invidious comparison that lurked behind his words.

Here was intellectual life, he thought, and here was beauty, warm and wonderful as he had never dreamed it could be. He forgot himself and stared at her with hungry eyes.

Here was something to live for, to win to, to fight for—ay, and die for. The books were true. There were such women in the world. She was one of them. She lent wings to his imagination, and great, luminous canvases spread themselves before him whereon loomed vague, gigantic figures of love and romance, and of heroic deeds for woman's sake—for a pale woman, a flower of gold.

—from *Martin Eden*

"Now go ahead, Joe. You were speaking to me a moment ago in conundrums, and you have aroused my curiosity to a most uncomfortable degree."

Whereupon Joe sat down and told what had happened—all that had happened—from Monday night to that very moment. Each little incident he related—every detail—not forgetting his conversations with 'Frisco Kid nor his plans concerning him. His face flushed and he was carried away with the excitement of the narrative, while Mr. Bronson was almost as eager, urging him on whenever he slackened his pace, but otherwise remaining silent.

"So you see," Joe concluded, "it could n't possibly have turned out any better."

"Ah, well," Mr. Bronson deliberated judiciously, "it may be so, and then again it may not."

"I don't see it." Joe felt sharp disappointment at his father's qualified approval. It seemed to him that the return of the safe merited something stronger.

That Mr. Bronson fully comprehended the way Joe felt about it was clearly in evidence, for he went on: "As to the matter of the safe, all hail to you, Joe! Credit, and plenty of it, is your due. Mr. Tate and myself have already spent five hundred dollars in attempting to recover it. So important was it that we have also offered five thousand dollars reward, and but this morning were considering the advisability of increasing the amount. But, my son,"—Mr. Bronson stood up, resting a hand affectionately on his boy's shoulder—"there are certain things in this world which are of still greater importance than gold, or papers which represent what gold may buy. How about *yourself*? That's the point. Will you sell the best possibilities of your life right now for a million dollars?"

Joe shook his head.

"As I said, that's the point. A human life the money of the world cannot buy; nor can it redeem one which is misspent; nor can it make full and complete and beautiful a life which is dwarfed and warped and ugly. How about yourself? What is to be the effect of all these strange adventures on your life—*your* life, Joe? Are you going to pick yourself up to-morrow and try it over again? or the next day? or the day after? Do you understand? Why, Joe, do you think for one moment that I would place against the best value of my son's life the paltry value of a safe? And can I say, until time has told me, whether this trip of yours could not possibly have been better? Such an experience is as potent for evil as for good. One dollar is exactly like another—there are many in the world: but no Joe is like my Joe, nor can there be any others in the world to take his place. Don't you see, Joe? Don't you understand?"

—from *The Cruise of the Dazzler*

"I wonder if you ever miss what you've missed," she told him. "Did you ever, once in your life, turn yourself loose and rip things up by the roots? Did you ever once get drunk? Or smoke yourself black in the face? Or dance a hoe-down on the ten commandments? Or stand up on your hind legs and wink like a good fellow at God?"

The fascination of the light for the grey cub increased from day to day. He was perpetually departing on yard-long adventures toward the cave's entrance, and as perpetually being driven back. Only he did not know it for an entrance. He did not know anything about entrances—passages whereby one goes from one place to another place. He did not know any other place, much less of a way to get there. So to him the entrance of the cave was a wall—a wall of light. As the sun was to the outside dweller, this wall was to him the sun of his world. It attracted him as a candle attracts a moth. He was always striving to attain it. The life that was so swiftly expanding within him, urged him continually toward the wall of light. The life that was within him knew that it was the one way out, the way he was predestined to tread. But he himself did not know anything about it. He did not know there was any outside at all.

There was one strange thing about this wall of light. His father (he had already come to recognize his father as the one other dweller in the world, a creature like his mother, who slept near the light and was a bringer of meat)—his father had a way of walking right into the white far wall and disappearing. The grey cub could not understand this. Though never permitted by his mother to approach that wall, he had approached the other walls, and encountered hard obstruction on the end of his tender nose. This hurt. And after several such adventures, he left the walls alone. Without thinking about it, he accepted this disappearing into the wall as a peculiarity of his father, as milk and half-digested meat were peculiarities of his mother.

THE PULL OF THE WILD

And closely akin to the visions of the hairy man was the call still sounding in the depths of the forest. It filled him with a great unrest and strange desires. It caused him to feel a vague, sweet gladness, and he was aware of wild yearnings and stirrings for he knew not what. Sometimes he pursued the call into the forest, looking for it as though it were a tangible thing, barking softly or defiantly, as the mood might dictate. He would thrust his nose into the cool wood moss, or into the black soil where long grasses grew, and snort with joy at the fat earth smells; or he would crouch for hours, as if in concealment, behind fungus-covered trunks of fallen trees, wide-eyed and wide-eared to all that moved and sounded about him. It might be, lying thus, that he hoped to surprise this call he could not understand. But he did not know why he did these various things. He was impelled to do them, and did not reason about them at all.

Irresistible impulses seized him. He would be lying in camp, dozing lazily in the heat of the day, when suddenly his head would lift and his ears cock up, intent and listening, and he would spring to his feet and dash away, and on and on, for hours, through the forest aisles . . . But especially he loved to run in the dim twilight of the summer midnights, listening to the subdued and sleepy murmurs of the forest, reading signs and sounds as man may read a book, and seeking for the mysterious something that called—called, waking or sleeping, at all times, for him to come.

My first thought was that a man who had come through a collision and rubbed shoulders with death merited more attention than I received.

—from *The Sea-Wolf*

I was not as other men—most other men; I knew what they did not know—the mystery of the heavens, that pointed out the way across the deep. And the taste of power I had received drove me on. I steered at the wheel long hours with one hand, and studied mystery with the other. By the end of the week. teaching myself, I was able to do divers things. For instance, I shot the North Star, at night, of course; got its altitude, corrected for index error, dip, etc., and found out latitude.

And this latitude agreed with the latitude of the previous noon corrected by dead reckoning up to that moment. Proud? Well, I was even prouder with my next miracle. I was going to turn in at nine o'clock. I worked out the problem, self-instructed, and learned what star of the first magnitude would be passing the meridian around half-past eight. This star proved to be Alpha Crucis. I had never heard of the star before. I looked it up on the star map. It was one of the stars of the Southern Cross. What! thought I; have we been sailing with the Southern Cross in the sky of nights and never known it? Dolts that we are? Gudgeons and moles! I couldn't believe it. I went over the problem again, and verified it. Charmian had the wheel from eight till ten that evening. I hold her to keep her eyes open and look due south for the Southern Cross. And when the stars came out, there shone the Southern Cross low on the horizon. Proud? No medicine man nor high priest was ever prouder. Furthermore, with the prayer-wheel I shot Alpha Crucis and from its altitude worked out our latitude. And still furthermore, I shot the North Star, too, and it agreed with what had been told me by the Southern Cross. Proud? Why the language of the stars was mine, and I listened and heard them telling me my way over the deep.

—from *The Cruise of the* Snark

Dark spruce forest frowned on either side the frozen waterway. The trees had been stripped by a recent wind of their white covering of frost, and they seemed to lean towards each other, black and ominous, in the fading light. A vast silence reigned over the land. The land itself was a desolation, lifeless, without movement, so lone and cold that the spirit of it was not even that of sadness. There was a hint in it of laughter, but of a laughter more terrible than any sadness—a laughter that was mirthless as the smile of the sphinx, a laughter cold as the frost and partaking of the grimness of infallibility. It was the masterful and incommunicable wisdom of eternity laughing at the futility of life and the effort of life. It was the Wild, the savage, frozen-hearted Northland Wild.

But there *was* life, abroad in the land and defiant. Down the frozen waterway toiled a string of wolfish dogs. Their bristly fur was rimed with frost. Their breath froze in the air as it left their mouths, spouting forth in spumes of vapour that settled upon the hair of their bodies and formed into crystals of frost. Leather harness was on the dogs, and leather traces attached them to a sled which dragged along behind. The sled was without runners. It was made of stout birch-bark, and its full surface rested on the snow. The front end of the sled was turned up, like a scroll, in order to force down and under the bore of soft snow that surged like a wave before it. On the sled, securely lashed, was a long and narrow oblong box. There were other things on the sled—blankets, an axe, and a coffee-pot and frying-pan; but prominent, occupying most of the space, was the long and narrow oblong box.

In advance of the dogs, on wide snow-shoes, toiled a man. At the rear of the sled toiled a second man. On the sled, in the box, lay a third man whose toil was over,—a man whom the Wild had conquered and beaten down until he would never move nor struggle again. It is not the way of the Wild to like movement. Life is an offence to it, for life is movement; and the Wild aims always to destroy movement. It freezes the water to prevent it running to the sea; it drives the sap out of the trees till they are frozen to their mighty hearts; and most ferociously and terribly of all does the Wild harry and crush into submission man—man who is the most restless of life, ever in revolt against the dictum that all movement must in the end come to the cessation of movement.

—from *White Fang*

The Wild still lingered in him and the wolf in him merely slept.

But there were other forces at work in the cub, the greatest of which was growth. Instinct and law demanded of him obedience. But growth demanded disobedience. His mother and fear impelled him to keep away from the white wall. Growth is life, and life is for ever destined to make for light. So there was no damming up the tide of life that was rising within him—rising with every mouthful of meat he swallowed, with every breath he drew. In the end, one day, fear and obedience were swept away by the rush of life, and the cub straddled and sprawled toward the entrance.

Unlike any other wall with which he had had experience, this wall seemed to recede from him as he approached. No hard surface collided with the tender little nose he thrust out tentatively before him. The substance of the wall seemed as permeable and yielding as light. And as condition, in his eyes, had the seeming of form, so he entered into what had been wall to him and bathed in the substance that composed it.

It was bewildering. He was sprawling through solidity. And ever the light grew brighter. Fear urged him to go back, but growth drove him on. Suddenly he found himself at the mouth of the cave. The wall, inside which he had thought himself, as suddenly leaped back before him to an immeasurable distance. The light had become painfully bright. He was dazzled by it. Likewise he was made dizzy by this abrupt and tremendous extension of space. Automatically, his eyes were adjusting themselves to the brightness, focusing themselves to meet the increased distance of objects. At first, the wall had leaped beyond his vision. He now saw it again; but it had taken upon itself a remarkable remoteness. Also, its appearance had changed. It was now a variegated wall, composed of the trees that fringed the stream, the opposing mountain that towered above the trees, and the sky that out-towered the mountain.

I chanced the chest and the slow-beating heart. The quick compulsion of my will was rewarded. I no longer had chest nor heart. I was only a mind, a soul, a consciousness—call it what you will—incorporate in a nebulous brain that, while it still centered inside my skull, was expanded, and was continuing to expand, beyond my skull.

And then, with flashings of light, I was off and away. At a bound I had vaulted prison roof and California sky, and was among the stars. I say "stars" advisedly. I walked among the stars. I was a child. I was clad in frail, fleece-like, delicate-coloured robes that shimmered in the cool starlight. These robes, of course, were based upon my boyhood observance of circus actors and my boyhood conception of the garb of young angels.

Nevertheless, thus clad, I trod interstellar space, exalted by the knowledge that I was bound on vast adventure, where, at the end, I would find all the cosmic formulae and have made clear to me the ultimate secret of the universe.

He worked slowly and carefully, keenly aware of his danger. Gradually, as the flame grew stronger, he increased the size of the twigs with which he fed it. He squatted in the snow, pulling the twigs out from their entanglement in the brush and feeding directly to the flame. He knew there must be no failure. When it is seventy-five below zero, a man must not fail in his first attempt to build a fire—that is, if his feet are wet. If his feet are dry, and he fails, he can run along the trail for half a mile and restore his circulation. But the circulation of wet and freezing feet cannot be restored by running when it is seventy-five below. No matter how fast he runs, the wet feet will freeze the harder.

—from "To Build a Fire"

The afternoon wore on, and with the awe, born of the White Silence, the voiceless travelers bent to their work. Nature has many tricks wherewith she convinces man of his finity—the ceaseless flow of the tides, the fury of the storm, the shock of the earthquake, the long roll of heaven's artillery—but the most tremendous, the most stupefying of all, is the passive phase of the White Silence. All movement ceases, the sky clears, the heavens are as brass; the slightest whisper seems sacrilege, and man becomes timid, affrighted at the sound of his own voice.

Sole speck of life journeying across the ghostly wastes of a dead world, he trembles at his audacity, realizes that his is a maggot's life, nothing more. Strange thoughts arise unsummoned, and the mystery of all things strives for utterance. And the fear of death, of God, of the universe, comes over him—the hope of the Resurrection and the Life, the yearning for immortality, the vain striving of the imprisoned essence—it is then, if ever, man walks alone with God.

—from "The White Silence"

ESSAYS AND EXCERPTS

"Small Boat Sailing," from *The Human Drift and a Collection of Stories*

A sailor is born, not made. And by "sailor" is meant, not the average efficient and hopeless creature who is found to-day in the forecastle of deepwater ships, but the man who will take a fabric compounded of wood and iron and rope and canvas and compel it to obey his will on the surface of the sea. Barring captains and mates of big ships, the small-boat sailor is the real sailor. He knows—he must know—how to make the wind carry his craft from one given point to another given point. He must know about tides and rips and eddies, bar and channel markings, and day and night signals; he must be wise in weather-lore; and he must be sympathetically familiar with the peculiar qualities of his boat which differentiate it from every other boat that was ever built and rigged. He must know how to gentle her about, as one instance of a myriad, and to fill her on the other tack without deadening her way or allowing her to fall off too far.

The deepwater sailor of to-day needs know none of these things. And he doesn't. He pulls and hauls as he is ordered, swabs decks, washes paint, and chips iron-rust. He knows nothing, and cares less. Put him in a small boat and he is helpless. He will cut an even better figure on the hurricane deck of a horse.

I shall never forget my child-astonishment when I first encountered one of these strange beings. He was a runaway English sailor. I was a lad of twelve, with a decked-over, fourteen-foot, centre-board skiff which I had taught myself to sail. I sat at his feet as at the feet of a god, while he discoursed of strange lands and peoples, deeds of violence, and hair-raising gales at sea. Then, one day, I took him for a sail. With all the trepidation of the veriest little amateur, I hoisted sail and got under way. Here was a man, looking on critically, I was sure, who knew more in one second about boats and the water than I could ever know. After an interval, in which I exceeded myself, he took the tiller and the sheet. I sat on the little thwart amidships, open-mouthed, prepared to learn what real sailing was. My mouth remained open, for I learned what a real sailor was in a small boat. He couldn't trim the sheet to save himself, he nearly capsized several times in squalls, and, once again, by blunderingly jibing over; he didn't know what a centre-board was for, nor did he know that in running a boat before the wind one must sit in the middle instead of on the side; and finally, when we came back to the wharf, he ran the skiff in full tilt, shattering her nose and carrying away the mast-step. And yet he was a really truly sailor fresh from the vasty deep.

Which points my moral. A man can sail in the forecastles of big ships all his life and never know what real sailing is. From the time I was twelve, I listened to the lure of the sea. When I was fifteen I was captain and owner of an oyster-pirate sloop. By the time I was sixteen I was sailing in scow-schooners, fishing salmon with the Greeks up the Sacramento River, and serving as sailor on the Fish Patrol. And I was a good sailor, too, though all my cruising had been on San Francisco Bay and the rivers tributary to it. I had never been on the ocean in my life.

Then, the month I was seventeen, I signed before the mast as an able seaman on a three-top-mast schooner bound on a seven-months' cruise across the Pacific and back again. As my shipmates promptly informed me, I had had my nerve with me to sign on as able seaman. Yet behold, I WAS an able seaman. I had graduated from the right school. It took no more than minutes to learn the names and uses of the few new ropes. It was simple. I did not do things blindly. As a small-boat sailor I had learned to reason out and know the WHY of everything. It is true, I had to learn how to steer by compass, which took maybe half a minute; but when it came to steering "full-and-by" and "close-and-by," I could beat the average of my shipmates, because that was the very way I had always sailed. Inside fifteen minutes I could box the compass around and back again. And there was little else to learn during that seven-months' cruise, except fancy rope-sailorising, such as the more complicated lanyard knots and the making of various kinds of sennit and rope-mats. The point of all of which is that it is by means of small-boat sailing that the real sailor is best schooled.

And if a man is a born sailor, and has gone to the school of the sea, never in all his life can he get away from the sea again. The salt of it is in his bones as well as his nostrils, and the sea will call to him until he dies. Of late years, I have found easier ways of earning a living. I have quit the forecastle for keeps, but always I come back to the sea. In my case it is usually San Francisco Bay, than which no lustier, tougher, sheet of water can be found for small-boat sailing.

It really blows on San Francisco Bay. During the winter, which is the best cruising season, we have southeasters, south-westers, and occasional howling northers. Throughout the summer we have what we call the "sea-breeze," an unfailing wind off the Pacific that on most afternoons in the week blows what the Atlantic Coast yachtsmen would name a gale. They are always surprised by the small spread of canvas our yachts carry. Some of them, with schooners they have sailed around the Horn, have looked proudly at their own lofty sticks and huge spreads, then patronisingly and even pityingly at ours. Then, perchance, they have joined in a club cruise from San Francisco to Mare Island. They found the morning run up the Bay delightful. In the afternoon, when the brave west wind ramped across San

Pablo Bay and they faced it on the long beat home, things were somewhat different. One by one, like a flight of swallows, our more meagrely sparred and canvassed yachts went by, leaving them wallowing and dead and shortening down in what they called a gale but which we called a dandy sailing breeze. The next time they came out, we would notice their sticks cut down, their booms shortened, and their after-leeches nearer the luffs by whole cloths.

As for excitement, there is all the difference in the world between a ship in trouble at sea, and a small boat in trouble on landlocked water. Yet for genuine excitement and thrill, give me the small boat. Things happen so quickly, and there are always so few to do the work—and hard work, too, as the small-boat sailor knows. I have toiled all night, both watches on deck, in a typhoon off the coast of Japan, and been less exhausted than by two hours' work at reefing down a thirty-foot sloop and heaving up two anchors on a lee shore in a screaming south-easter.

Hard work and excitement? Let the wind baffle and drop in a heavy tide-way just as you are sailing your little sloop through a narrow draw-bridge. Behold your sails, upon which you are depending, flap with sudden emptiness, and then see the impish wind, with a haul of eight points, fill your jib aback with a gusty puff. Around she goes, and sweeps, not through the open draw, but broadside on against the solid piles. Hear the roar of the tide, sucking through the trestle. And hear and see your pretty, fresh-painted boat crash against the piles. Feel her stout little hull give to the impact. See the rail actually pinch in. Hear your canvas tearing, and see the black, square-ended timbers thrusting holes through it. Smash! There goes your topmast stay, and the topmast reels over drunkenly above you. There is a ripping and crunching. If it continues, your starboard shrouds will be torn out. Grab a rope—any rope—and take a turn around a pile. But the free end of the rope is too short. You can't make it fast, and you hold on and wildly yell for your one companion to get a turn with another and longer rope. Hold on! You hold on till you are purple in the face, till it seems your arms are dragging out of their sockets, till the blood bursts from the ends of your fingers. But you hold, and your partner gets the longer rope and makes it fast. You straighten up and look at your hands. They are ruined. You can scarcely relax the crooks of the fingers. The pain is sickening. But there is no time. The skiff, which is always perverse, is pounding against the barnacles on the piles which threaten to scrape its gunwale off. It's drop the peak! Down jib! Then you run lines, and pull and haul and heave, and exchange unpleasant remarks with the bridge-tender who is always willing to meet you more than half way in such repartee. And finally, at the end of an hour, with aching back, sweat-soaked shirt, and slaughtered hands, you are through and swinging along on the placid, beneficent tide between narrow banks where the cattle stand knee-deep and gaze wonderingly at you. Excitement! Work! Can you beat it in a calm day on the deep sea?

I've tried it both ways. I remember labouring in a fourteen days' gale off the coast of New Zealand. We were a tramp collier, rusty and battered, with six thousand tons of coal in our hold. Life lines were stretched fore and aft; and on our weather side, attached to smokestack guys and rigging, were huge rope-nettings, hung there for the purpose of breaking the force of the seas and so saving our mess-room doors. But the doors were smashed and the mess-rooms washed out just the same. And yet, out of it all, arose but the one feeling, namely, of monotony.

In contrast with the foregoing, about the liveliest eight days of my life were spent in a small boat on the west coast of Korea. Never mind why I was thus voyaging up the Yellow Sea during the month of February in below-zero weather. The point is that I was in an open boat, a sampan, on a rocky coast where there were no light-houses and where the tides rip. We did not speak each other's language. Yet there was nothing monotonous about that trip. Never shall I forget one particular cold bitter dawn, when, in the thick of driving snow, we took in sail and dropped our small anchor. The wind was howling out of the northwest, and we were on a lee shore. Ahead and astern, all escape was cut off by rocky headlands, against whose bases burst the unbroken seas. To windward a short distance, seen only between the snow-squalls, was a low rocky reef. It was this that inadequately protected us from the whole Yellow Sea that thundered in upon us.

The Japanese crawled under a communal rice mat and went to sleep. I joined them, and for several hours we dozed fitfully. Then a sea deluged us out with icy water, and we found several inches of snow on top the mat. The reef to windward was disappearing under the rising tide, and moment by moment the seas broke more strongly over the rocks. The fishermen studied the shore anxiously. So did I, and with a sailor's eye, though I could see little chance for a swimmer to gain that surf-hammered line of rocks. I made signs toward the headlands on either flank. The Japanese shook their heads. I indicated that dreadful lee shore. Still they shook their heads and did nothing. My conclusion was that they were paralysed by the hopelessness of the situation. Yet our extremity increased with every minute, for the rising tide was robbing us of the reef that served as buffer. It soon became a case of swamping at our anchor. Seas were splashing on board in growing volume, and we baled constantly. And still my fishermen crew eyed the surf-battered shore and did nothing.

At last, after many narrow escapes from complete swamping, the fishermen got into action. All hands tailed on to the anchor and hove it up. For'ard, as the boat's head paid off, we set a patch of sail about the size of a flour-sack. And we headed straight for shore. I unlaced my shoes, unbottoned my great-coat and coat, and was ready to make a quick partial strip a minute or so before we struck. But we didn't strike, and, as we rushed in, I saw the beauty of the situation. Before us opened a narrow channel, frilled at its mouth with breaking seas. Yet, long before, when I had scanned the shore closely, there had been no such channel. I HAD FORGOTTEN THE THIRTY-FOOT TIDE. And it was for this tide that the Japanese had so precariously waited. We ran the frill of breakers, curved into a tiny sheltered bay where the water was scarcely flawed by the gale, and landed on a beach where the salt sea of the last tide lay frozen in long curving lines. And this was one gale of three in the course of those eight days in the sampan. Would it have been beaten on a ship? I fear me the ship would have gone aground on the outlying reef and that its people would have been incontinently and monotonously drowned.

There are enough surprises and mishaps in a three-days' cruise in a small boat to supply a great ship on the ocean for a full year. I remember, once, taking out on her trial trip a little thirty-footer I had just bought. In six days we had two stiff blows, and, in addition, one proper southwester and one ripsnorting southeaster. The slight intervals between these blows were dead calms. Also, in the six days, we were aground three times. Then, too, we tied up to the bank in the Sacramento River, and, grounding by an accident on the steep slope on a falling tide, nearly turned a side somersault down the bank. In a stark calm and heavy tide in the Carquinez Straits, where anchors skate on the channel-scoured bottom, we were sucked against a big dock and smashed and bumped down a quarter of a mile of its length before we could get clear. Two hours afterward, on San Pablo Bay, the wind was piping up and we were reefing down. It is no fun to pick up a skiff adrift in a heavy sea and gale. That was our next task, for our skiff, swamping, parted both towing painters we had bent on. Before we recovered it we had nearly killed ourselves with exhaustion, and we certainly had strained the sloop in every part from keelson to truck. And to cap it all, coming into our home port, beating up the narrowest part of the San Antonio Estuary, we had a shave of inches from collision with a big ship in tow of a tug. I have sailed the ocean in far larger craft a year at a time, in which period occurred no such chapter of moving incident.

After all, the mishaps are almost the best part of small-boat sailing. Looking back, they prove to be punctuations of joy.

At the time they try your mettle and your vocabulary, and may make you so pessimistic as to believe that God has a grudge against you—but afterward, ah, afterward, with what pleasure you remember them and with what gusto do you relate them to your brother skippers in the fellowhood of small-boat sailing!

A narrow, winding slough; a half tide, exposing mud surfaced with gangrenous slime; the water itself filthy and discoloured by the waste from the vats of a near-by tannery; the marsh grass on either side mottled with all the shades of a decaying orchid; a crazy, ramshackled, ancient wharf; and at the end of the wharf a small, white-painted sloop. Nothing romantic about it. No hint of adventure. A splendid pictorial argument against the alleged joys of small-boat sailing. Possibly that is what Cloudesley and I thought, that sombre, leaden morning as we turned out to cook breakfast and wash decks. The latter was my stunt, but one look at the dirty water overside and another at my fresh-painted deck, deterred me. After breakfast, we started a game of chess. The tide continued to fall, and we felt the sloop begin to list. We played on until the chess men began to fall over. The list increased, and we went on deck. Bow-line and stern-line were drawn taut. As we looked the boat listed still farther with an abrupt jerk. The lines were now very taut.

"As soon as her belly touches the bottom she will stop," I said.

Cloudesley sounded with a boat-hook along the outside.

"Seven feet of water," he announced. "The bank is almost up and down. The first thing that touches will be her mast when she turns bottom up."

An ominous, minute snapping noise came from the stern-line. Even as we looked, we saw a strand fray and part. Then we jumped. Scarcely had we bent another line between the stern and the wharf, when the original line parted. As we bent another line for'ard, the original one there crackled and parted. After that, it was an inferno of work and excitement.

We ran more and more lines, and more and more lines continued to part, and more and more the pretty boat went over on her side. We bent all our spare lines; we unrove sheets and halyards; we used our two-inch hawser; we fastened lines part way up the mast, half way up, and everywhere else. We toiled and sweated and enounced our mutual and sincere conviction that God's grudge still held against us. Country yokels came down on the wharf and sniggered at us. When Cloudesley let a coil of rope slip down the inclined deck into the vile slime and fished it out with seasick countenance, the yokels sniggered louder and it was all I could do to prevent him from climbing up on the wharf and committing murder.

By the time the sloop's deck was perpendicular, we had unbent the boom-lift from below, made it fast to the wharf, and, with the other end fast nearly to the mast-head, heaved it taut with block and tackle. The lift was of steel wire. We were confident that it could stand the strain, but we doubted the holding-power of the stays that held the mast.

The tide had two more hours to ebb (and it was the big run-out), which meant that five hours must elapse ere the returning tide would give us a chance to learn whether or not the sloop would rise to it and right herself.

The bank was almost up and down, and at the bottom, directly beneath us, the fast-ebbing tide left a pit of the vilest, illest-smelling, illest-appearing muck to be seen in many a day's ride. Said Cloudesley to me gazing down into it:

"I love you as a brother. I'd fight for you. I'd face roaring lions, and sudden death by field and flood. But just the same, don't you fall into that." He shuddered nauseously. "For if you do, I haven't the grit to pull you out. I simply couldn't. You'd be awful. The best I could do would be to take a boat-hook and shove you down out of sight."

We sat on the upper side-wall of the cabin, dangled our legs down the top of the cabin, leaned our backs against the deck, and played chess until the rising tide and the block and tackle on the boom-lift enabled us to get her on a respectable keel again. Years afterward, down in the South Seas, on the island of Ysabel, I was caught in a similar predicament. In order to clean her copper, I had careened the *Snark* broadside on to the beach and outward. When the tide rose, she refused to rise. The water crept in through the scuppers, mounted over the rail, and the level of the ocean slowly crawled up the slant of the deck. We battened down the engine-room hatch, and the sea rose to it and over it and climbed perilously near to the cabin companion-way and skylight.

We were all sick with fever, but we turned out in the blazing tropic sun and toiled madly for several hours. We carried our heaviest lines ashore from our mast-heads and heaved with our heaviest purchase until everything crackled including ourselves. We would spell off and lie down like dead men, then get up and heave and crackle again. And in the end, our lower rail five feet under water and the wavelets lapping the companion-way combing, the sturdy little craft shivered and shook herself and pointed her masts once more to the zenith.

There is never lack of exercise in small-boat sailing, and the hard work is not only part of the fun of it, but it beats the doctors. San Francisco Bay is no mill pond. It is a large and draughty and variegated piece of water. I remember, one winter evening, trying to enter the mouth of the Sacramento. There was a freshet on the river, the flood tide from the bay had been beaten back into a strong ebb, and the lusty west wind died down with the sun. It was just sunset, and with a fair to middling breeze, dead aft, we stood still in the rapid current. We were squarely in the mouth of the river; but there was no anchorage and we drifted backward, faster and faster, and dropped anchor outside as the last breath of wind left us. The night came on, beautiful and warm and starry. My one companion cooked supper, while on deck I put everything in shape Bristol fashion. When we turned in at nine o'clock the weather-promise was excellent. (If I had carried a barometer I'd have known better.)

By two in the morning our shrouds were thrumming in a piping breeze, and I got up and gave her more scope on her hawser. Inside another hour there was no doubt that we were in for a southeaster.

It is not nice to leave a warm bed and get out of a bad anchorage in a black blowy night, but we arose to the occasion, put in two reefs, and started to heave up. The winch was old, and the strain of the jumping head sea was too much for it. With the winch out of commission, it was impossible to heave up by hand. We knew, because we tried it and slaughtered our hands. Now a sailor hates to lose an anchor. It is a matter of pride. Of course, we could have buoyed ours and slipped it. Instead, however, I gave her still more hawser, veered her, and dropped the second anchor.

There was little sleep after that, for first one and then the other of us would be rolled out of our bunks. The increasing size of the seas told us we were dragging, and when we struck the scoured channel we could tell by the feel of it that our two anchors were fairly skating across. It was a deep channel, the farther edge of it rising steeply like the wall of a canyon, and when our anchors started up that wall they hit in and held.

Yet, when we fetched up, through the darkness we could hear the seas breaking on the solid shore astern, and so near was it that we shortened the skiff's painter.

Daylight showed us that between the stern of the skiff and destruction was no more than a score of feet. And how it did blow! There were times, in the gusts, when the wind must have approached a velocity of seventy or eighty miles an hour. But the anchors held, and so nobly that our final anxiety was that the for'ard bitts would be jerked clean out of the boat. All day the sloop alternately ducked her nose under and sat down on her stern; and it was not till late afternoon that the storm broke in one last and worst mad gust. For a full five minutes an absolute dead calm prevailed, and then, with the suddenness of a thunderclap, the wind snorted out of the southwest—a shift of eight points and a boisterous gale. Another night of it was too much for us, and we hove up by hand in a cross head-sea. It was not stiff work. It was heart-breaking. And I know we were both near to crying from the hurt and the exhaustion. And when we did get the first anchor up-and-down we couldn't break it out. Between seas we snubbed her nose down to it, took plenty of turns, and stood clear as she jumped. Almost everything smashed and parted except the anchor-hold. The chocks were jerked out, the rail torn off, and the very covering-board splintered, and still the anchor held. At last, hoisting the reefed main-sail and slacking off a few of the hard-won feet of the chain, we sailed the anchor out. It was nip and tuck, though, and there were times when the boat was knocked down flat. We repeated the manoeuvre with the remaining anchor, and in the gathering darkness fled into the shelter of the river's mouth.

I was born so long ago that I grew up before the era of gasolene. As a result, I am old-fashioned. I prefer a sail-boat to a motor-boat, and it is my belief that boat-sailing is a finer, more difficult, and sturdier art than running a motor. Gasolene engines are becoming fool-proof, and while it is unfair to say that any fool can run an engine, it is fair to say that almost any one can. Not so, when it comes to sailing a boat. More skill, more intelligence, and a vast deal more training are necessary. It is the finest training in the world for boy and youth and man.If the boy is very small, equip him with a small, comfortable skiff. He will do the rest. He won't need to be taught. Shortly he will be setting a tiny leg-of-mutton and steering with an oar. Then he will begin to talk keels and centreboards and want to take his blankets out and stop aboard all night.

But don't be afraid for him. He is bound to run risks and encounter accidents. Remember, there are accidents in the nursery as well as out on the water. More boys have died from hot-house culture than have died on boats large and small; and more boys have been made into strong and reliant men by boat-sailing than by lawn-croquet and dancing-school.

And once a sailor, always a sailor. The savour of the salt never stales. The sailor never grows so old that he does not care to go back for one more wrestling bout with wind and wave. I know it of myself. I have turned rancher, and live beyond sight of the sea. Yet I can stay away from it only so long. After several months have passed, I begin to grow restless. I find myself day-dreaming over incidents of the last cruise, or wondering if the striped bass are running on Wingo Slough, or eagerly reading the newspapers for reports of the first northern flights of ducks. And then, suddenly, there is a hurried pack of suit-cases and overhauling of gear, and we are off for Vallejo where the little Roamer lies, waiting, always waiting, for the skiff to come alongside, for the lighting of the fire in the galley-stove, for the pulling off of gaskets, the swinging up of the mainsail, and the rat-tat-tat of the reef-points, for the heaving short and the breaking out, and for the twirling of the wheel as she fills away and heads up Bay or down.

Excerpt from *The Sea Wolf*

I could not feel the full force of the wind, for we were running with it; but from my lofty perch I looked down as though outside the *Ghost* and apart from her, and saw the shape of her outlined sharply against the foaming sea as she tore along instinct with life. Sometimes she would lift and send across some great wave, burying her starboard-rail from view, and covering her deck to the hatches with the boiling ocean. At such moments, starting from a windward roll, I would go flying through the air with dizzying swiftness, as though I clung to the end of a huge, inverted pendulum, the arc of which, between the greater rolls, must have been seventy feet or more. Once, the terror of this giddy sweep overpowered me, and for a while I clung on, hand and foot, weak and trembling, unable to search the sea for the missing boats or to behold aught of the sea but that which roared beneath and strove to overwhelm the *Ghost*.

But the thought of the men in the midst of it steadied me, and in my quest for them I forgot myself. For an hour I saw nothing but the naked, desolate sea. And then, where a vagrant shaft of sunlight struck the ocean and turned its surface to wrathful silver, I caught a small black speck thrust skyward for an instant and swallowed up. I waited patiently. Again the tiny point of black projected itself through the wrathful blaze a couple of points off our port-bow. I did not attempt to shout, but communicated the news to Wolf Larsen by waving my arm. He changed the course, and I signalled affirmation when the speck showed dead ahead.

It grew larger, and so swiftly that for the first time I fully appreciated the speed of our flight. Wolf Larsen motioned for me to come down, and when I stood beside him at the wheel gave me instructions for heaving to.

Expect all hell to break loose," he cautioned me, "but don't mind it. Yours is to do your own work and to have Cooky stand by the fore-sheet."

I managed to make my way forward, but there was little choice of sides, for the weather-rail seemed buried as often as the lee. Having instructed Thomas Mugridge as to what he was to do, I clambered into the fore-rigging a few feet. The boat was now very close, and I could make out plainly that it was lying head to wind and sea and dragging on itsmast and sail, which had been thrown overboard and made to serve as a sea-anchor. The three men were bailing. Each rolling mountain whelmed them from view, and I would wait with sickening anxiety, fearing that they would never appear again. Then, and with black suddenness, the boat would shoot clear through the foaming crest, bow pointed to the sky, and the whole length of her bottom showing, wet and dark, till she seemed on end. There would be a fleeting glimpse of the three men flinging water in frantic haste, when she would topple over and fall into the yawning valley, bow down and showing her full inside length to the stern upreared almost directly above the bow. Each time that she reappeared was a miracle.

The *Ghost* suddenly changed her course, keeping away, and it came to me with a shock that Wolf Larsen was giving up the rescue as impossible. Then I realized that he was preparing to heave to, and dropped to the deck to be in readiness. We were now dead before the wind, the boat far away and abreast of us. I felt an abrupt easing of the schooner, a loss for the moment of all strain and pressure, coupled with a swift acceleration of speed. She was rushing around on her heel into the wind.

As she arrived at right angles to the sea, the full force of the wind (from which we had hitherto run away) caught us. I was unfortunately and ignorantly facing it. It stood up against me like a wall, filling my lungs with air which I could not expel. And as I choked and strangled, and as the *Ghost* wallowed for an instant, broadside on and rolling straight over and far into the wind, I beheld a huge sea rise far above my head. I turned aside, caught my breath, and looked again. The wave over-topped the *Ghost*, and I gazed sheer up and into it. A shaft of sunlight smote the over-curl, and I caught a glimpse of translucent, rushing green, backed by a milky smother of foam.

Then it descended, pandemonium broke loose, everything happened at once. I was struck a crushing, stunning blow, nowhere in particular and yet everywhere. My hold had been broken loose, I was under water, and the thought passed through my mind that this was the terrible thing of which I had heard, the being swept in the trough of the sea. My body struck and pounded as it was dashed helplessly along and turned over and over, and when I could hold my breath no longer, I breathed the stinging salt water into my lungs. But through it all I clung to the one idea—I must get the jib backed over to windward. I had no fear of death. I had no doubt but that I should come through somehow. And as this idea of fulfilling Wolf Larsen's order persisted in my dazed consciousness, I seemed to see him standing at the wheel in the midst of the wild welter, pitting his will against the will of the storm and defying it.

I brought up violently against what I took to be the rail, breathed, and breathed the sweet air again. I tried to rise, but struck my head and was knocked back on hands and knees. By some freak of the waters I had been swept clear under the forecastle-head and into the eyes. As I scrambled out on all fours, I passed over the body of Thomas Mugridge, who lay in a groaning heap. There was no time to investigate. I must get the jib backed over.

When I emerged on deck it seemed that the end of everything had come. On all sides there was a rending and crashing of wood and steel and canvas. The *Ghost* was being wrenched and torn to fragments. The foresail and fore-topsail, emptied of the wind by the manœuvre, and with no one to bring in the sheet in time, were thundering into ribbons, the heavy boom threshing and splintering from rail to rail. The air was thick with flying wreckage, detached ropes and stays were hissing and coiling like snakes, and down through it all crashed the gaff of the foresail.

The spar could not have missed me by many inches, while it spurred me to action. Perhaps the situation was not hopeless.

I remembered Wolf Larsen's caution. He had expected all hell to break loose, and here it was. And where was he? I caught sight of him toiling at the main-sheet, heaving it in and flat with his tremendous muscles, the stern of the schooner lifted high in the air and his body outlined against a white surge of sea sweeping past. All this, and more—a whole world of chaos and wreck—in possibly fifteen seconds I had seen and heard and grasped.

I did not stop to see what had become of the small boat, but sprang to the jib-sheet. The jib itself was beginning to slap, partially filling and emptying with sharp reports; but with a turn of the sheet and the application of my whole strength each time it slapped, I slowly backed it. This I know: I did my best. I pulled till I burst open the ends of all my fingers; and while I pulled, the flying-jib and staysail split their cloths apart and thundered into nothingness.

Still I pulled, holding what I gained each time with a double turn until the next slap gave me more. Then the sheet gave with greater ease, and Wolf Larsen was beside me, heaving in alone while I was busied taking up the slack.

"Make fast!" he shouted. "And come on!"

As I followed him, I noted that in spite of rack and ruin a rough order obtained. The *Ghost* was hove to. She was still in working order, and she was still working. Though the rest of her sails were gone, the jib, backed to windward, and the mainsail hauled down flat, were themselves holding, and holding her bow to the furious sea as well.

I looked for the boat, and, while Wolf Larsen cleared the boat-tackles, saw it lift to leeward on a big sea an not a score of feet away. And, so nicely had he made his calculation, we drifted fairly down upon it, so that nothing remained to do but hook the tackles to either end and hoist it aboard. But this was not done so easily as it is written.

In the bow was Kerfoot, Oofty-Oofty in the stern, and Kelly amidships. As we drifted closer the boat would rise on a wave while we sank in the trough, till almost straight above me I could see the heads of the three men craned overside and looking down. Then, the next moment, we would lift and soar upward while they sank far down beneath us. It seemed incredible that the next surge should not crush the *Ghost* down upon the tiny eggshell.

But, at the right moment, I passed the tackle to the Kanaka, while Wolf Larsen did the same thing forward to Kerfoot. Both tackles were hooked in a trice, and the three men, deftly timing the roll, made a simultaneous leap aboard the schooner. As the *Ghost* rolled her side out of water, the boat was lifted snugly against her, and before the return roll came, we had heaved it in over the side and turned it bottom up on the deck. I noticed blood spouting from Kerfoot's left hand. In some way the third finger had been crushed to a pulp. But he gave no sign of pain, and with his single right hand helped us lash the boat in its place.

"Stand by to let that jib over, you Oofty!" Wolf Larsen commanded, the very second we had finished with the boat. "Kelly, come aft and slack off the main-sheet! You, Kerfoot, go for'ard and see what's become of Cooky! Mr. Van Weyden, run aloft again, and cut away any stray stuff on your way!"

And having commanded, he went aft with his peculiar tigerish leaps to the wheel. While I toiled up the fore-shrouds the *Ghost* slowly paid off. This time, as we went into the trough of the sea and were swept, there were no sails to carry away. And, halfway to the crosstrees and flattened against the rigging by the full force of the wind so that it would have been impossible for me to have fallen, the *Ghost* almost on her beam-ends and the masts parallel with the water, I looked, not down, but at almost right angles from the perpendicular, to the deck of the *Ghost*. But I saw, not the deck, but where the deck should have been, for it was buried beneath a wild tumbling of water. Out of this water I could see the two masts rising, and that was all. The *Ghost*, for the moment, was buried beneath the sea. As she squared off more and more, escaping from the side pressure, she righted herself and broke her deck, like a whale's back, through the ocean surface.

Then we raced, and wildly, across the wild sea, the while I hung like a fly in the crosstrees and searched for the other boats. In half-an-hour I sighted the second one, swamped and bottom up, to which were desperately clinging Jock Horner, fat Louis, and Johnson. This time I remained aloft, and Wolf Larsen succeeded in heaving to without being swept. As before, we drifted down upon it. Tackles were made fast and lines flung to the men, who scrambled aboard like monkeys. The boat itself was crushed and splintered against the schooner's side as it came inboard; but the wreck was securely lashed, for it could be patched and made whole again.

Once more the *Ghost* bore away before the storm, this time so submerging herself that for some seconds I thought she would never reappear. Even the wheel, quite a deal higher than the waist, was covered and swept again and again. At such moments I felt strangely alone with God, alone with him and watching the chaos of his wrath. And then the wheel would reappear, and Wolf Larsen's broad shoulders, his hands gripping the spokes and holding the schooner to the course of his will, himself an earth-god, dominating the storm, flinging its descending waters from him and riding it to his own ends. And oh, the marvel of it! the marvel of it! That tiny men should live and breathe and work, and drive so frail a contrivance of wood and cloth through so tremendous an elemental strife.

As before, the *Ghost* swung out of the trough, lifting her deck again out of the sea, and dashed before the howling blast. It was now half-past five, and half-an-hour later, when the last of the day lost itself in a dim and furious twilight, I sighted a third boat. It was bottom up, and there was no sign of its crew. Wolf Larsen repeated his manœuvre, holding off and then rounding up to windward and drifting down upon it. But this time he missed by forty feet, the boat passing astern.

"Number four boat!" Oofty-Oofty cried, his keen eyes reading its number in the one second when it lifted clear of the foam, and upside down.

It was Henderson's boat and with him had been lost Holyoak and Williams, another of the deep-water crowd. Lost they indubitably were; but the boat remained, and Wolf Larsen made one more reckless effort to recover it. I had come down to the deck, and I saw Horner and Kerfoot vainly protest against the attempt.

"By God, I'll not be robbed of my boat by any storm that ever blew out of hell!" he shouted, and though we four stood with our heads together that we might hear, his voice seemed faint and far, as though removed from us an immense distance.

"Mr. Van Weyden!" he cried, and I heard through the tumult as one might hear a whisper. "Stand by that jib with Johnson and Oofty! The rest of you tail aft to the mainsheet! Lively now! or I'll sail you all into Kingdom Come! Understand?"

And when he put the wheel hard over and the *Ghost*'s bow swung off, there was nothing for the hunters to do but obey and make the best of a risky chance. How great the risk I realized when I was once more buried beneath the pounding seas and clinging for life to the pinrail at the foot of the foremast. My fingers were torn loose, and I swept across to the side and over the side into the sea. I could not swim, but before I could sink I was swept back again. A strong hand gripped me, and when the *Ghost* finally emerged, I found that I owed my life to Johnson. I saw him looking anxiously about him, and noted that Kelly, who had come forward at the last moment, was missing.

This time, having missed the boat, and not being in the same position as in the previous instances, Wolf Larsen was compelled to resort to a different manœuvre. Running off before the wind with everything to starboard, he came about, and returned close-hauled on the port tack.

"Grand!" Johnson shouted in my ear, as we successfully came through the attendant deluge, and I knew he referred, not to Wolf Larsen's seamanship, but to the performance of the *Ghost* herself.

It was now so dark that there was no sign of the boat; but Wolf Larsen held back through the frightful turmoil as if guided by unerring instinct. This time, though we were continually half-buried, there was no trough in which to be swept, and we drifted squarely down upon the upturned boat, badly smashing it as it was heaved inboard.

Two hours of terrible work followed, in which all hands of us—two hunters, three sailors, Wolf Larsen and I—reefed, first one and then the other, the jib and mainsail. Hove to under this short canvas, our decks were comparatively free of water, while the *Ghost* bobbed and ducked amongst the combers like a cork.

To Build a Fire

Day had broken cold and gray, exceedingly cold and gray, when the man turned aside from the main Yukon trail and climbed the high earth-bank, where a dim and little-travelled trail led eastward through the fat spruce timberland. It was a steep bank, and he paused for breath at the top, excusing the act to himself by looking at his watch. It was nine o'clock. There was no sun nor hint of sun, though there was not a cloud in the sky. It was a clear day, and yet there seemed an intangible pall over the face of things, a subtle gloom that made the day dark, and that was due to the absence of sun. This fact did not worry the man. He was used to the lack of sun. It had been days since he had seen the sun, and he knew that a few more days must pass before that cheerful orb, due south, would just peep above the sky-line and dip immediately from view.

The man flung a look back along the way he had come. The Yukon lay a mile wide and hidden under three feet of ice. On top of this ice were as many feet of snow. It was all pure white, rolling in gentle undulations where the ice-jams of the freeze-up had formed. North and south, as far as his eye could see, it was unbroken white, save for a dark hair-line that curved and twisted from around the spruce-covered island to the south, and that curved and twisted away into the north, where it disappeared behind another spruce-covered island. This dark hair-line was the trail—the main trail—that led south five hundred miles to the Chilcoot Pass, Dyea, and salt water; and that led north seventy miles to Dawson, and still on to the north a thousand miles to Nulato, and finally to St. Michael on Bering Sea, a thousand miles and half a thousand more.

But all this—the mysterious, far-reaching hair-line trail, the absence of sun from the sky, the tremendous cold, and the strangeness and weirdness of it all—made no impression on the man. It was not because he was long used to it. He was a newcomer in the land, a *chechaquo*, and this was his first winter. The trouble with him was that he was without imagination. He was quick and alert in the things of life, but only in the things, and not in the significances. Fifty degrees below zero meant eighty-odd degrees of frost. Such fact impressed him as being cold and uncomfortable, and that was all. It did not lead him to meditate upon his frailty as a creature of temperature, and upon man's frailty in general, able only to live within certain narrow limits of heat and cold; and from there on it did not lead him to the conjectural field of immortality and man's place in the universe. Fifty degrees below zero stood for a bite of frost that hurt and that must be guarded against by the use of mittens, ear-flaps, warm moccasins, and thick socks. Fifty degrees below zero was to him just precisely fifty degrees below zero. That there should be anything more to it than that was a thought that never entered his head.

As he turned to go on, he spat speculatively. There was a sharp, explosive crackle that startled him. He spat again. And again, in the air, before it could fall to the snow, the spittle crackled. He knew that at fifty below spittle crackled on the snow, but this spittle had crackled in the air. Undoubtedly it was colder than fifty below—how much colder he did not know. But the temperature did not matter. He was bound for the old claim on the left fork of Henderson Creek, where the boys were already. They had come over across the divide from the Indian Creek country, while he had come the roundabout way to take a look at the possibilities of getting out logs in the spring from the islands in the Yukon. He would be in to camp by six o'clock; a bit after dark, it was true, but the boys would be there, a fire would be going, and a hot supper would be ready. As for lunch, he pressed his hand against the protruding bundle under his jacket. It was also under his shirt, wrapped up in a handkerchief and lying against the naked skin. It was the only way to keep the biscuits from freezing. He smiled agreeably to himself as he thought of those biscuits, each cut open and sopped in bacon grease, and each enclosing a generous slice of fried bacon.

He plunged in among the big spruce trees. The trail was faint. A foot of snow had fallen since the last sled had passed over, and he was glad he was without a sled, travelling light. In fact, he carried nothing but the lunch wrapped in the handkerchief. He was surprised, however, at the cold. It certainly was cold, he concluded, as he rubbed his numb nose and cheek-bones with his mittened hand. He was a warm-whiskered man, but the hair on his face did not protect the high cheek-bones and the eager nose that thrust itself aggressively into the frosty air.

At the man's heels trotted a dog, a big native husky, the proper wolf-dog, gray-coated and without any visible or temperamental difference from its brother, the wild wolf. The animal was depressed by the tremendous cold. It knew that it was no time for travelling. Its instinct told it a truer tale than was told to the man by the man's judgment. In reality, it was not merely colder than fifty below zero; it was colder than sixty below, than seventy below. It was seventy-five below zero. Since the freezing-point is thirty-two above zero, it meant that one hundred and seven degrees of frost obtained. The dog did not know anything about thermometers. Possibly in its brain there was no sharp consciousness of a condition of very cold such as was in the man's brain. But the brute had its instinct.

It experienced a vague but menacing apprehension that subdued it and made it slink along at the man's heels, and that made it question eagerly every unwonted movement of the man as if expecting him to go into camp or to seek shelter somewhere and build a fire. The dog had learned fire, and it wanted fire, or else to burrow under the snow and cuddle its warmth away from the air.

The frozen moisture of its breathing had settled on its fur in a fine powder of frost, and especially were its jowls, muzzle, and eyelashes whitened by its crystalled breath. The man's red beard and mustache were likewise frosted, but more solidly, the deposit taking the form of ice and increasing with every warm, moist breath he exhaled. Also, the man was chewing tobacco, and the muzzle of ice held his lips so rigidly that he was unable to clear his chin when he expelled the juice. The result was that a crystal beard of the color and solidity of amber was increasing its length on his chin. If he fell down it would shatter itself, like glass, into brittle fragments. But he did not mind the appendage. It was the penalty all tobacco-chewers paid in that country, and he had been out before in two cold snaps. They had not been so cold as this, he knew, but by the spirit thermometer at Sixty Mile he knew they had been registered at fifty below and at fifty-five.

He held on through the level stretch of woods for several miles, crossed a wide flat of niggerheads, and dropped down a bank to the frozen bed of a small stream. This was Henderson Creek, and he knew he was ten miles from the forks. He looked at his watch. It was ten o'clock. He was making four miles an hour, and he calculated that he would arrive at the forks at half-past twelve. He decided to celebrate that event by eating his lunch there.

The dog dropped in again at his heels, with a tail drooping discouragement, as the man swung along the creek-bed. The furrow of the old sled-trail was plainly visible, but a dozen inches of snow covered the marks of the last runners. In a month no man had come up or down that silent creek. The man held steadily on. He was not much given to thinking, and just then particularly he had nothing to think about save that he would eat lunch at the forks and that at six o'clock he would be in camp with the boys. There was nobody to talk to; and, had there been, speech would have been impossible because of the ice-muzzle on his mouth. So he continued monotonously to chew tobacco and to increase the length of his amber beard.

Once in a while the thought reiterated itself that it was very cold and that he had never experienced such cold. As he walked along he rubbed his cheek-bones and nose with the back of his mittened hand. He did this automatically, now and again changing hands. But rub as he would, the instant he stopped his cheek-bones went numb, and the following instant the end of his nose went numb. He was sure to frost his cheeks; he knew that, and experienced a pang of regret that he had not devised a nose-strap of the sort Bud wore in cold snaps. Such a strap passed across the cheeks, as well, and saved them. But it didn't matter much, after all. What were frosted cheeks? A bit painful, that was all; they were never serious.

Empty as the man's mind was of thoughts, he was keenly observant, and he noticed the changes in the creek, the curves and bends and timber-jams, and always he sharply noted where he placed his feet. Once, coming around a bend, he shied abruptly, like a startled horse, curved away from the place where he had been walking, and retreated several paces back along the trail. The creek he knew was frozen clear to the bottom,—no creek could contain water in that arctic winter,—but he knew also that there were springs that bubbled out from the hillsides and ran along under the snow and on top the ice of the creek. He knew that the coldest snaps never froze these springs, and he knew likewise their danger. They were traps. They hid pools of water under the snow that might be three inches deep, or three feet. Sometimes a skin of ice half an inch thick covered them, and in turn was covered by the snow. Sometimes there were alternate layers of water and ice-skin, so that when one broke through he kept on breaking through for a while, sometimes wetting himself to the waist.

That was why he had shied in such panic. He had felt the give under his feet and heard the crackle of a snow-hidden ice-skin. And to get his feet wet in such a temperature meant trouble and danger. At the very least it meant delay, for he would be forced to stop and build a fire, and under its protection to bare his feet while he dried his socks and moccasins. He stood and studied the creek-bed and its banks, and decided that the flow of water came from the right. He reflected awhile, rubbing his nose and cheeks, then skirted to the left, stepping gingerly and testing the footing for each step. Once clear of the danger, he took a fresh chew of tobacco and swung along at his four-mile gait. In the course of the next two hours he came upon several similar traps. Usually the snow above the hidden pools had a sunken, candied appearance that advertised the danger. Once again, however, he had a close call; and once, suspecting danger, he compelled the dog to go on in front. The dog did not want to go. It hung back until the man shoved it forward, and then it went quickly across the white, unbroken surface. Suddenly it broke through, floundered to one side, and got away to firmer footing. It had wet its forefeet and legs, and almost immediately the water that clung to it turned to ice. It made quick efforts to lick the ice off its legs, then dropped down in the snow and began to bite out the ice that had formed between the toes. This was a matter of instinct. To permit the ice to remain would mean sore feet. It did not know this. It merely obeyed the mysterious prompting that arose from the deep crypts of its being. But the man knew, having achieved a judgment on the subject, and he removed the mitten from his right hand and helped tear out the ice-particles. He did not expose his fingers more than a minute, and was astonished at the swift numbness that smote them. It certainly was cold. He pulled on the mitten hastily, and beat the hand savagely across his chest.

At twelve o'clock the day was at its brightest. Yet the sun was too far south on its winter journey to clear the horizon. The bulge of the earth intervened between it and Henderson Creek, where the man walked under a clear sky at noon and cast no shadow. At half-past twelve, to the minute, he arrived at the forks of the creek. He was pleased at the speed he had made. If he kept it up, he would certainly be with the boys by six. He unbuttoned his jacket and shirt and drew forth his lunch. The action consumed no more than a quarter of a minute, yet in that brief moment the numbness laid hold of the exposed fingers. He did not put the mitten on, but, instead, struck the fingers a dozen sharp smashes against his leg. Then he sat down on a snow-covered log to eat. The sting that followed upon the striking of his fingers against his leg ceased so quickly that he was startled. He had had no chance to take a bite of biscuit. He struck the fingers repeatedly and returned them to the mitten, baring the other hand for the purpose of eating. He tried to take a mouthful, but the ice-muzzle prevented. He had forgotten to build a fire and thaw out. He chuckled at his foolishness, and as he chuckled he noted the numbness creeping into the exposed fingers. Also, he noted that the stinging which had first come to his toes when he sat down was already passing away. He wondered whether the toes were warm or numb. He moved them inside the moccasins and decided that they were numb.

He pulled the mitten on hurriedly and stood up. He was a bit frightened. He stamped up and down until the stinging returned into the feet. It certainly was cold, was his thought. That man from Sulphur Creek had spoken the truth when telling how cold it sometimes got in the country. And he had laughed at him at the time! That showed one must not be too sure of things. There was no mistake about it, it *was* cold. He strode up and down, stamping his feet and threshing his arms, until reassured by the returning warmth. Then he got out matches and proceeded to make a fire.

From the undergrowth, where high water of the previous spring had lodged a supply of seasoned twigs, he got his fire-wood. Working carefully from a small beginning, he soon had a roaring fire, over which he thawed the ice from his face and in the protection of which he ate his biscuits. For the moment the cold of space was outwitted. The dog took satisfaction in the fire, stretching out close enough for warmth and far enough away to escape being singed.

When the man had finished, he filled his pipe and took his comfortable time over a smoke. Then he pulled on his mittens, settled the ear-flaps of his cap firmly about his ears, and took the creek trail up the left fork. The dog was disappointed and yearned back toward the fire. This man did not know cold. Possibly all the generations of his ancestry had been ignorant of cold, of real cold, of cold one hundred and seven degrees below freezing-point. But the dog knew; all its ancestry knew, and it had inherited the knowledge. And it knew that it was not good to walk abroad in such fearful cold. It was the time to lie snug in a hole in the snow and wait for a curtain of cloud to be drawn across the face of outer space whence this cold came. On the other hand, there was no keen intimacy between the dog and the man. The one was the toil-slave of the other, and the only caresses it had ever received were the caresses of the whip-lash and of harsh and menacing throat-sounds that threatened the whip-lash. So the dog made no effort to communicate its apprehension to the man. It was not concerned in the welfare of the man; it was for its own sake that it yearned back toward the fire. But the man whistled, and spoke to it with the sound of whip-lashes, and the dog swung in at the man's heels and followed after.

The man took a chew of tobacco and proceeded to start a new amber beard. Also, his moist breath quickly powdered with white his mustache, eyebrows, and lashes. There did not seem to be so many springs on the left fork of the Henderson, and for half an hour the man saw no signs of any. And then it happened. At a place where there were no signs, where the soft, unbroken snow seemed to advertise solidity beneath, the man broke through. It was not deep. He wet himself halfway to the knees before he floundered out to the firm crust.

He was angry, and cursed his luck aloud. He had hoped to get into camp with the boys at six o'clock, and this would delay him an hour, for he would have to build a fire and dry out his foot-gear. This was imperative at that low temperature—he knew that much; and he turned aside to the bank, which he climbed. On top, tangled in the underbrush about the trunks of several small spruce trees, was a high-water deposit of dry fire-wood—sticks and twigs, principally, but also larger portions of seasoned branches and fine, dry, last-year's grasses. He threw down several large pieces on top of the snow. This served for a foundation and prevented the young flame from drowning itself in the snow it otherwise would melt. The flame he got by touching a match to a small shred of birch-bark that he took from his pocket. This burned even more readily than paper. Placing it on the foundation, he fed the young flame with wisps of dry grass and with the tiniest dry twigs.

He worked slowly and carefully, keenly aware of his danger. Gradually, as the flame grew stronger, he increased the size of the twigs with which he fed it. He squatted in the snow, pulling the twigs out from their entanglement in the brush and feeding directly to the flame. He knew there must be no failure. When it is seventy-five below zero, a man must not fail in his first attempt to build a fire—that is, if his feet are wet. If his feet are dry, and he fails, he can run along the trail for half a mile and restore his circulation. But the circulation of wet and freezing feet cannot be restored by running when it is seventy-five below. No matter how fast he runs, the wet feet will freeze the harder.

All this the man knew. The old-timer on Sulphur Creek had told him about it the previous fall, and now he was appreciating the advice. Already all sensation had gone out of his feet. To build the fire he had been forced to remove his mittens, and the fingers had quickly gone numb. His pace of four miles an hour had kept his heart pumping blood to the surface of his body and to all the extremities. But the instant he stopped, the action of the pump eased down. The cold of space smote the unprotected tip of the planet, and he, being on that unprotected tip, received the full force of the blow. The blood of his body recoiled before it. The blood was alive, like the dog, and like the dog it wanted to hide away and cover itself up from the fearful cold. So long as he walked four miles an hour, he pumped that blood, willy-nilly, to the surface; but now it ebbed away and sank down into the recesses of his body. The extremities were the first to feel its absence. His wet feet froze the faster, and his exposed fingers numbed the faster, though they had not yet begun to freeze. Nose and cheeks were already freezing, while the skin of all his body chilled as it lost its blood.

But he was safe. Toes and nose and cheeks would be only touched by the frost, for the fire was beginning to burn with strength. He was feeding it with twigs the size of his finger. In another minute he would be able to feed it with branches the size of his wrist, and then he could remove his wet foot-gear, and, while it dried, he could keep his naked feet warm by the fire, rubbing them at first, of course, with snow. The fire was a success. He was safe. He remembered the advice of the old-timer on Sulphur Creek, and smiled.

The old-timer had been very serious in laying down the law that no man must travel alone in the Klondike after fifty below. Well, here he was; he had had the accident; he was alone; and he had saved himself. Those old-timers were rather womanish, some of them, he thought. All a man had to do was to keep his head, and he was all right. Any man who was a man could travel alone. But it was surprising, the rapidity with which his cheeks and nose were freezing. And he had not thought his fingers could go lifeless in so short a time. Lifeless they were, for he could scarcely make them move together to grip a twig, and they seemed remote from his body and from him. When he touched a twig, he had to look and see whether or not he had hold of it. The wires were pretty well down between him and his finger-ends.

All of which counted for little. There was the fire, snapping and crackling and promising life with every dancing flame. He started to untie his moccasins. They were coated with ice; the thick German socks were like sheaths of iron halfway to the knees; and the moccasin strings were like rods of steel all twisted and knotted as by some conflagration. For a moment he tugged with his numb fingers, then, realizing the folly of it, he drew his sheath-knife.

But before he could cut the strings, it happened. It was his own fault or, rather, his mistake. He should not have built the fire under the spruce tree. He should have built it in the open. But it had been easier to pull the twigs from the brush and drop them directly on the fire. Now the tree under which he had done this carried a weight of snow on its boughs. No wind had blown for weeks, and each bough was fully freighted. Each time he had pulled a twig he had communicated a slight agitation to the tree—an imperceptible agitation, so far as he was concerned, but an agitation sufficient to bring about the disaster. High up in the tree one bough capsized its load of snow. This fell on the boughs beneath, capsizing them. This process continued, spreading out and involving the whole tree. It grew like an avalanche, and it descended without warning upon the man and the fire, and the fire was blotted out! Where it had burned was a mantle of fresh and disordered snow.

The man was shocked. It was as though he had just heard his own sentence of death. For a moment he sat and stared at the spot where the fire had been. Then he grew very calm. Perhaps the old-timer on Sulphur Creek was right. If he had only had a trail-mate he would have been in no danger now. The trail-mate could have built the fire. Well, it was up to him to build the fire over again, and this second time there must be no failure. Even if he succeeded, he would most likely lose some toes. His feet must be badly frozen by now, and there would be some time before the second fire was ready.

Such were his thoughts, but he did not sit and think them. He was busy all the time they were passing through his mind. He made a new foundation for a fire, this time in the open, where no treacherous tree could blot it out. Next, he gathered dry grasses and tiny twigs from the high-water flotsam. He could not bring his fingers together to pull them out, but he was able to gather them by the handful. In this way he got many rotten twigs and bits of green moss that were undesirable, but it was the best he could do. He worked methodically, even collecting an armful of the larger branches to be used later when the fire gathered strength. And all the while the dog sat and watched him, a certain yearning wistfulness in its eyes, for it looked upon him as the fire-provider, and the fire was slow in coming.

When all was ready, the man reached in his pocket for a second piece of birch-bark. He knew the bark was there, and, though he could not feel it with his fingers, he could hear its crisp rustling as he fumbled for it. Try as he would, he could not clutch hold of it. And all the time, in his consciousness, was the knowledge that each instant his feet were freezing. This thought tended to put him in a panic, but he fought against it and kept calm. He pulled on his mittens with his teeth, and threshed his arms back and forth, beating his hands with all his might against his sides. He did this sitting down, and he stood up to do it; and all the while the dog sat in the snow, its wolf-brush of a tail curled around warmly over its forefeet, its sharp wolf-ears pricked forward intently as it watched the man. And the man, as he beat and threshed with his arms and hands, felt a great surge of envy as he regarded the creature that was warm and secure in its natural covering.

After a time he was aware of the first faraway signals of sensation in his beaten fingers. The faint tingling grew stronger till it evolved into a stinging ache that was excruciating, but which the man hailed with satisfaction. He stripped the mitten from his right hand and fetched forth the birch-bark. The exposed fingers were quickly going numb again. Next he brought out his bunch of sulphur matches. But the tremendous cold had already driven the life out of his fingers. In his effort to separate one match from the others, the whole bunch fell in the snow. He tried to pick it out of the snow, but failed. The dead fingers could neither touch nor clutch. He was very careful. He drove the thought of his freezing feet, and nose, and cheeks, out of his mind, devoting his whole soul to the matches. He watched, using the sense of vision in place of that of touch, and when he saw his fingers on each side the bunch, he closed them—that is, he willed to close them, for the wires were down, and the fingers did not obey. He pulled the mitten on the right hand, and beat it fiercely against his knee. Then, with both mittened hands, he scooped the bunch of matches, along with much snow, into his lap. Yet he was no better off.

After some manipulation he managed to get the bunch between the heels of his mittened hands. In this fashion he carried it to his mouth. Thc icc crackled and snapped when by a violent effort he opened his mouth. He drew the lower jaw in, curled the upper lip out of the way, and scraped the bunch with his upper teeth in order to separate a match. He succeeded in getting one, which he dropped on his lap. He was no better off. He could not pick it up. Then he devised a way. He picked it up in his teeth and scratched it on his leg. Twenty times he scratched before he succeeded in lighting it. As it flamed he held it with his teeth to the birch-bark. But the burning brimstone went up his nostrils and into his lungs, causing him to cough spasmodically. The match fell into the snow and went out.

The old-timer on Sulphur Creek was right, he thought in the moment of controlled despair that ensued: after fifty below, a man should travel with a partner. He beat his hands, but failed in exciting any sensation. Suddenly he bared both hands, removing the mittens with his teeth. He caught the whole bunch between the heels of his hands. His arm-muscles not being frozen enabled him to press the hand-heels tightly against the matches. Then he scratched the bunch along his leg. It flared into flame, seventy sulphur matches at once! There was no wind to blow them out. He kept his head to one side to escape the strangling fumes, and held the blazing bunch to the birch-bark. As he so held it, he became aware of sensation in his hand. His flesh was burning. He could smell it. Deep down below the surface he could feel it. The sensation developed into pain that grew acute. And still he endured it, holding the flame of the matches clumsily to the bark that would not light readily because his own burning hands were in the way, absorbing most of the flame.

At last, when he could endure no more, he jerked his hands apart. The blazing matches fell sizzling into the snow, but the birch-bark was alight. He began laying dry grasses and the tiniest twigs on the flame. He could not pick and choose, for he had to lift the fuel between the heels of his hands. Small pieces of rotten wood and green moss clung to the twigs, and he bit them off as well as he could with his teeth. He cherished the flame carefully and awkwardly. It meant life, and it must not perish. The withdrawal of blood from the surface of his body now made him begin to shiver, and he grew more awkward. A large piece of green moss fell squarely on the little fire. He tried to poke it out with his fingers, but his shivering frame made him poke too far, and he disrupted the nucleus of the little fire, the burning grasses and tiny twigs separating and scattering. He tried to poke them together again, but in spite of the tenseness of the effort, his shivering got away with him, and the twigs were hopelessly scattered. Each twig gushed a puff of smoke and went out. The fire-provider had failed. As he looked apathetically about him, his eyes chanced on the dog, sitting across the ruins of the fire from him, in the snow, making restless, hunching movements, slightly lifting one forefoot and then the other, shifting its weight back and forth on them with wistful eagerness.

The sight of the dog put a wild idea into his head. He remembered the tale of the man, caught in a blizzard, who killed a steer and crawled inside the carcass, and so was saved. He would kill the dog and bury his hands in the warm body until the numbness went out of them. Then he could build another fire. He spoke to the dog, calling it to him; but in his voice was a strange note of fear that frightened the animal, who had never known the man to speak in such way before. Something was the matter, and its suspicious nature sensed danger—it knew not what danger, but somewhere, somehow, in its brain arose an apprehension of the man. It flattened its ears down at the sound of the man's voice, and its restless, hunching movements and the liftings and shiftings of its forefeet became more pronounced; but it would not come to the man. He got on his hands and knees and crawled toward the dog. This unusual posture again excited suspicion, and the animal sidled mincingly away.

The man sat up in the snow for a moment and struggled for calmness. Then he pulled on his mittens, by means of his teeth, and got upon his feet. He glanced down at first in order to assure himself that he was really standing up, for the absence of sensation in his feet left him unrelated to the earth. His erect position in itself started to drive the webs of suspicion from the dog's mind; and when he spoke peremptorily, with the sound of whip-lashes in his voice, the dog rendered its customary allegiance and came to him. As it came within reaching distance, the man lost his control. His arms flashed out to the dog, and he experienced genuine surprise when he discovered that his hands could not clutch, that there was neither bend nor feeling in the fingers. He had forgotten for the moment that they were frozen and that they were freezing more and more. All this happened quickly, and before the animal could get away, he encircled its body with his arms. He sat down in the snow, and in this fashion held the dog, while it snarled and whined and struggled.

But it was all he could do, hold its body encircled in his arms and sit there. He realized that he could not kill the dog. There was no way to do it. With his helpess hands he could neither draw nor hold his sheath-knife nor throttle the animal. He released it, and it plunged wildly away, with tail between its legs, and still snarling. It halted forty feet away and surveyed him curiously, with ears sharply pricked forward. The man looked down at his hands in order to locate them, and found them hanging on the ends of his arms. It struck him as curious that one should have to use his eyes in order to find out where his hands were. He began threshing his arms back and forth, beating the mittened hands against his sides. He did this for five minutes, violently, and his heart pumped enough blood up to the surface to put a stop to his shivering. But no sensation was aroused in the hands. He had an impression that they hung like weights on the ends of his arms, but when he tried to run the impression down, he could not find it.

A certain fear of death, dull and oppressive, came to him. This fear quickly became poignant as he realized that it was no longer a mere matter of freezing his fingers and toes, or of losing his hands and feet, but that it was a matter of life and death with the chances against him. This threw him into a panic, and he turned and ran up the creek-bed along the old, dim trail. The dog joined in behind and kept up with him. He ran blindly, without intention, in fear such as he had never known in his life. Slowly, as he ploughed and floundered through the snow, he began to see things again—the banks of the creek, the old timber-jams, the leafless aspens, and the sky. The running made him feel better. He did not shiver. Maybe, if he ran on, his feet would thaw out; and, anyway, if he ran far enough, he would reach camp and the boys. Without doubt he would lose some fingers and toes and some of his face; but the boys would take care of him, and save the rest of him when he got there. And at the same time there was another thought in his mind that said he would never get to the camp and the boys; that it was too many miles away, that the freezing had too great a start on him, and that he would soon be stiff and dead. This thought he kept in the background and refused to consider. Sometimes it pushed itself forward and demanded to be heard, but he thrust it back and strove to think of other things.

It struck him as curious that he could run at all on feet so frozen that he could not feel them when they struck the earth and took the weight of his body. He seemed to himself to skim along above the surface, and to have no connection with the earth. Somewhere he had once seen a winged Mercury, and he wondered if Mercury felt as he felt when skimming over the earth.

His theory of running until he reached camp and the boys had one flaw in it: he lacked the endurance. Several times he stumbled, and finally he tottered, crumpled up, and fell. When he tried to rise, he failed. He must sit and rest, he decided, and next time he would merely walk and keep on going. As he sat and regained his breath, he noted that he was feeling quite warm and comfortable. He was not shivering, and it even seemed that a warm glow had come to his chest and trunk. And yet, when he touched his nose or cheeks, there was no sensation. Running would not thaw them out. Nor would it thaw out his hands and feet. Then the thought came to him that the frozen portions of his body must be extending. He tried to keep this thought down, to forget it, to think of something else; he was aware of the panicky feeling that it caused, and he was afraid of the panic. But the thought asserted itself, and persisted, until it produced a vision of his body totally frozen. This was too much, and he made another wild run along the trail. Once he slowed down to a walk, but the thought of the freezing extending itself made him run again.

And all the time the dog ran with him, at his heels. When he fell down a second time, it curled its tail over its forefeet and sat in front of him, facing him, curiously eager and intent. The warmth and security of the animal angered him, and he cursed it till it flattened down its ears appeasingly. This time the shivering came more quickly upon the man. He was losing in his battle with the frost. It was creeping into his body from all sides. The thought of it drove him on, but he ran no more than a hundred feet, when he staggered and pitched headlong. It was his last panic. When he had recovered his breath and control, he sat up and entertained in his mind the conception of meeting death with dignity. However, the conception did not come to him in such terms. His idea of it was that he had been making a fool of himself, running around like a chicken with its head cut off—such was the simile that occurred to him. Well, he was bound to freeze anyway, and he might as well take it decently. With this new-found peace of mind came the first glimmerings of drowsiness. A good idea, he thought, to sleep off to death. It was like taking an anaesthetic. Freezing was not so bad as people thought. There were lots worse ways to die.

He pictured the boys finding his body next day. Suddenly he found himself with them, coming along the trail and looking for himself. And, still with them, he came around a turn in the trail and found himself lying in the snow. He did not belong with himself any more, for even then he was out of himself, standing with the boys and looking at himself in the snow. It certainly was cold, was his thought. When he got back to the States he could tell the folks what real cold was. He drifted on from this to a vision of the old-timer on Sulphur Creek. He could see him quite clearly, warm and comfortable, and smoking a pipe.

“You were right, old hoss; you were right,” the man mumbled to the old-timer of Sulphur Creek.

Then the man drowsed off into what seemed to him the most comfortable and satisfying sleep he had ever known. The dog sat facing him and waiting. The brief day drew to a close in a long, slow twilight. There were no signs of a fire to be made, and, besides, never in the dog’s experience had it known a man to sit like that in the snow and make no fire. As the twilight drew on, its eager yearning for the fire mastered it, and with a great lifting and shifting of forefeet, it whined softly, then flattened its ears down in anticipation of being chidden by the man. But the man remained silent. Later, the dog whined loudly. And still later it crept close to the man and caught the scent of death. This made the animal bristle and back away. A little longer it delayed, howling under the stars that leaped and danced and shone brightly in the cold sky. Then it turned and trotted up the trail in the direction of the camp it knew, where were the other food-providers and fire-providers.

—*End*